ADVANCED PRAISE FOR *THE LITTLEST SAILBOAT*

Theresa Contaxis has written a delightful book that all ages can enjoy. It is about the struggle of growing up and maturing which we all go through as we learn how to be free of the hurtful barnacles we collect along the way. It's about how our attitude determines everything that happens to us, up to the point where we can sail through life regardless of the storms, the reefs, and the unexpected waves. It is about learning how to get more in touch with "the wind" i.e., Spirit, and how we can sail through life doing good and receiving good. Thanks, Theresa, for the lovely read.

~ Dr. Jon Mundy, author of *Living A Course in Miracles*

The Littlest Sailboat takes us on a life journey from fear and insecurity to self-love and inner peace. With childlike playfulness, this book goes to the core of emotional issues that we all must face and overcome. Spiritually, it represents the ultimate human journey.

**~ Rev. Susanna Stefanachi Macomb, author of *Joining Hands and Hearts,* and *Bless This Child*
Interfaith Minister, Peace Advocate, Author, Speaker, Counselor, Artist**

THE LITTLEST

SAILBOAT

A JOURNEY OF THE SOUL

THE LITTLEST SAILBOAT
A JOURNEY OF THE SOUL

Theresa Contaxis

IPBooks Inc
Infinite Possibilities
New York ● https://ipbooks.net

THE LITTLEST SAILBOAT
A Journey of the Soul

Published by IPBooks Inc
Queens, New York, 11104, USA
Online at www.IPBooks.net

Copyright © 2021 by Theresa Contaxis
All rights reserved. This book may not be reproduced, transmitted, or stored, in whole or in part by any means, including graphic, electronic, or mechanical without the express permission of the author and/or publisher, except in the case of brief quotations, embodied in critical articles and reviews.
ISBN: 978-1-949093-98-8

Editing, Cover Design, Layout, Typesetting & Digital Art by lisa roma

Cover & Interior Watercolor Illustrations by Jennifer Anne Contaxis
Copyright © 2021 by Jennifer Anne Contaxis

Dedication

I dedicate this book to my husband, Dean. Calling him husband is not nearly enough.
He is a partner in this life, who has always supported my journey, no matter what
direction it took. Though he did not always understand, he was always accepting.
He is my "Joseph" who has always cared for and watched over me.
I thank him from the depths of my heart.

"The only relationship which holds any value at all is your relationship with God, your creative Source, the depth of the Ocean. For when that is in alignment, all of your creations, your choices for relationships, and how you will be within them, will flow effortlessly from that alignment.

Therefore, seek first the Kingdom, and all these things will be added unto you."

--"The Way of the Heart" from the Shanti Christo Foundation

*A*s I sail out of the harbor, I look forward to where I will be heading next, no longer afraid of what is in store for me.

Where is the Wind taking me now? Don't know, don't care.
Wherever the Wind takes me is perfect.

Oh, I'm sorry! I didn't realize you haven't yet heard of me.
I thought you knew my story. Let me introduce myself.

I am The Littlest Sailboat.

I was created approximately
six decades ago, in Earth
years, but was told I have
been around much longer.

I was told I had come out of
the depths of the Ocean, with
a perfect visual
representation of myself.

When I first came into this vessel, I had a beautiful white sail
and a purple hull. I was always around older boats who tried to
help me grow until I was ready to go out on my own.

I had no idea what that meant, or what I was to do.

I became fearful because I thought I had to do this Journey all alone. I was told to work hard so that I would be better than the other boats.

That was truly frightening because I saw many boats that looked bigger and better than me.

And I didn't even have a motor!

I became jealous of many boats. I would look at them and always think they were more special than me.

I saw steamboats and tugboats and other boats.

My very favorite was the cruise liner.

Although the cruise liners were my favorite, I thought all the boats were more special compared to me.

But mostly, I wanted to *be* a cruise liner.

Still, every time I looked in the mirror, I would simply see a little sailboat.

I had gone through many experiences that made me feel small.
Not little, just small. Bigger boats would bully me, leading me
to believe that I was small, or less than seaworthy. I started
feeling I had nothing to offer.

What was a little sailboat like me to do?

I was told by one of the older boats, "You could be anything you want to be if you just work hard enough."
So, I decided I would be a cruise liner! In my eyes, a cruise liner always seemed to get everything they wanted.

(I did not realize they were just like me.)

Cruise liners also desired what they thought other boats had. The cruise liner would get so tired because it had to work extra hard at looking special all the time!

(Something I did not realize.)

I was not as fond of destroyers—just the name was scary! They were always ready to attack any other boat.

In some ways the submarines were even worse. You would think the submarine was your friend and then the next thing you knew, a torpedo was coming right at you!

That would really hurt my feelings.

I also saw rowboats, which I was happy to meet.

I thought I was special compared to a rowboat. I liked having rowboats in my life, not only because I felt special, but I was able to tell THEM what to do.

(I did not even think of the fact that I was treating them as the bigger boats had treated me.)

Later on in my Journey, I realized words like anger, fear, jealousy, greed and shame began to appear on my sail. Actually, it was not the words themselves but the energy the words carried. I held that energy within me, instead of allowing it to just pass by.

My hull was no longer bright and shiny. Barnacles appeared there as well, with words like depression, loneliness and despair. Though I tried to remove them, the barnacles clung tightly to my hull.

Like my sail, I did not let the energy of the words float by, as a cloud passes in the sky, and the emotions remained stuck within me.

I had a problem that other boats could see my sail getting sullied. I wanted it to appear as if my sail were unblemished.

I did not mind the barnacles as much because no one could see them as long as I stayed in the water.

(At least, that is what I thought).

So, here were all these big ships and me, the littlest sailboat.   I figured that if I were smarter than all the other boats, I would start feeling better about myself.

I decided to go to Boat School.

Once again, I met many boats. However, it was no different than before. I constantly complained that I wanted to be different, that I wanted to be special, like so many of the other boats.

I kept looking for something outside of myself to feel special, just wanting to feel loved.

Though I did well in Boat School, I did not feel special or smart.

My thinking was that if other boats thought I was smart they might look up to me and want to be around me.

I worked hard at being the best student in the school; but even achieving that goal, I felt empty inside.

While attending Boat School, I met this wonderful boat, and that became the best part of school.

We were always together (me and my special boat) and he wanted to make me happy. I became more interested in this beautiful boat than school. I was a wonderful student, but I just wanted to be with my favorite boat.

Finally, someone made me feel special. And I felt loved.

After school, I found a wonderful job where I was able to use
my education from the Boat School. The boats liked my work
and even seemed to like me.

Funny thing though, I did not feel smart, and I didn't like myself.
Inside I did not see what they saw, so I did my best to hide. I
did not let my Authentic Self shine.

Actually, I had thought my job was going to make me happy because everyone would look up to me. If I was really being honest with myself, I would have realized I was never truly in touch with my Authentic Self, because I was trying to find myself from the outside in, rather than the inside out. That's why I was still trying to be a cruise liner.

Then something changed.

My special boat and I started having baby boats come into our lives that needed care. I stopped my job and had no one praising me any longer. I felt lost.

Over time, something else began to happen.

I was becoming angrier. The depression was getting deeper,
and I felt lonely, unworthy and unloved.

My special sailboat was not doing things the way I thought they
needed to be done. He didn't even go where I wanted to go. He
would want to go where the Wind was taking him.

I would fight with the Wind, which was useless because I had
no motor and could only go where the Wind would take me.

This went on for years.

I started meeting other boats who were helping me to see myself differently, to see my true beauty.

There was this pontoon boat who loved herself and enjoyed Creation. She just loved to carry people around as she slowly motored around the lake. She told me she loved the joy she gave to the humans.

I admired that pontoon boat and wanted to be like her. Maybe, just maybe, if I acted like the pontoon boat, I would like myself.

Somehow, now, something had changed. I saw pontoon's inner beauty and how that beauty made life more enjoyable in the outside world.

I met other sailboats along my Journey, and I was jealous of them because they were bigger than me and *even* had *motors!*

During this time, more dark spots appeared on my sail, words like unworthiness. Other words on my sail were getting bigger and darker, like shame, and guilt.

The barnacles of depression and loneliness were growing larger as well.

I did not understand that by not embracing my emotions, I was adding to my pain.

As much as I did not like my dark sail, it was okay because so many sailboats had dark sails, and the bigger boats had lots of barnacles. Nonetheless, I still became jealous of what other boats had.

I saw that I was becoming greedy because I always wanted more. I was looking out into the world to find something to fill me up, to make me feel whole.

Over the years, I completely lost sight of who I was.

Did I ever really know? Perhaps not, since I was searching everywhere else but in the right place to find myself.

I decided to go for a sail to think about everything.

I did not want to be in pain anymore.

"There must be a better way," I told myself.

The Wind was blowing strong, but I did not want to go the way it was blowing.

I tried to go against the Wind, but all that fighting was just making me tired, frustrated and eventually so weak that I could not fight anymore.

I was so weak that I did not have the strength to move.

Suddenly, a big wave came and turned me over. I began to fill with water and was being swallowed up by the Ocean. But I was too exhausted to care.

To my surprise, a huge blast of Wind came and picked me up. I was so tired, I just slept. I am not even sure for how long.

When I awoke, the water was calm, and the Wind was blowing ever so gently.

Greed
Shame
Jealousy
dness
Anger

Within my hull there was some of the Ocean.

I thought, *"How interesting, having the water within me."*

I had been told before that I came from the depths of the Ocean, though that never seemed to make any sense to me. Yet, here I was, floating in the Ocean with some of the Ocean inside me. That had to mean something important, but I wasn't sure what.

So, I headed back to shore, knowing something had changed. My life seemed to be the same on the outside, I still had all the barnacles on me and a dirty sail, but something was different.

I desired to learn and understand more about the Ocean.

I never really thought about the Ocean, except when I needed it to get me from place to place. I began going out on the Ocean more often, by myself. Ten minutes slowly increased to twenty. One day, I happened to glance at my hull. To my surprise, a barnacle had loosened. It was not gone, but it was no longer tight on my hull.

When I tried to remove the barnacles by myself, I could not. Now, a barnacle had loosened on its own! I did not understand how that happened. I was not trying to do anything, except to spend more time with the Ocean.

The next time I went out for one of my daily trips on the Ocean, I saw a human on the dock, crying. Wanting to investigate, I sailed into port and asked the human what was wrong.

The human wanted to visit their sick father. I thought, *I have things to do, but something about this human's pain touches me.* I decided to take the human to see their father.

My hope was that the Wind would be blowing in the right direction for me to take them there. I was doubtful because the Wind never blew in the direction that I wanted it to blow.

39

To my surprise, however, the Wind was blowing in the perfect direction! It took some time, but we arrived.

The human expressed so much gratitude. What was more interesting was what I felt inside. I felt grateful that I was able to help. The human gave me as much as I gave the human.

As I prepared to leave the dock, I was concerned that I would not make it back home. I needed the Wind to work for me in the opposite direction. But the Wind never seemed to cooperate with me, why would it do so now?

As I left the harbor, the Wind suddenly changed direction!

The trip home was gratifying, peaceful, and satisfying.

All my senses were completely filled with joy.

When I awoke the next morning, I looked down at my hull, and the barnacle named "selfishness" had fallen off.

My sail had a white spot that I had not seen in years. Actually, I did not notice with all the time I was spending on the Ocean, that quite a few barnacles had loosened.

The barnacles like "greed" and "despair" were now looser.
On top of that, my sail was getting brighter.

As I met other boats, I was no longer secretly wishing that I was more like them. On top of that, I was not as fearful of destroyers and submarines. I was learning to see their beauty as well. We actually became friendly. They were not scary, the way I used to think of them.

No longer was I looking so hard for their barnacles.

(I am not saying I stopped seeing them altogether, but I didn't look for them to make me feel better.)

My special boat also seemed to be different. I was no longer upset when he chose not to do what I wanted. I started to see things differently. Instead of feeling he did not help me enough, I saw how hard he worked for me and the baby boats.

I had a newfound peace and self-acceptance, which I wanted to understand more deeply. I remembered the pontoon boat. That pontoon just seemed so happy with everything exactly as it was. Maybe she could help me.

(And so, the Journey began ... or, so I thought. Later on, I would realize that the Journey had started a long time before.)

I found someone to get me back to the lake and I went to search for pontoon boat.

I did not find pontoon for some time, and I was growing frustrated. To my surprise, a new barnacle was starting to form on my hull. I wondered, *"Do my emotions have anything to do with these barnacles?"*

But there was no time to think about that at the moment.

I had to find pontoon boat.

I still was not aware that when I did not let my emotions pass, like a cloud in the sky, it would affect my sail and hull.

After looking for days, I finally found pontoon boat.

I began asking her lots of questions. Pontoon answered my questions, but I did not understand. I felt as if she were speaking a different language.

I had read many books and had several degrees from Boat School, yet I did not fully comprehend her teachings.

Why was this so difficult for me to understand?

I stayed with pontoon boat for a couple of weeks, feeling rejuvenated and renewed, not quite knowing why. It suddenly dawned on me that it was not *what* pontoon boat was saying, but the *Love* she was saying it *with*.

Even though she learned much about my life, which led to all the barnacles and the dirty sail, I was not being judged. Instead, I was being Embraced and Loved.

I was not Embraced because of my outer self.

I was Embraced for my Inner Self, and for my Light.

This Acceptance felt new and healing to me.

The lessons pontoon taught me led to new experiences, which gave me a deeper knowing.

This knowing led me to Embrace and Accept myself.

No longer was I comparing myself to others. (At least not nearly as often.) I realized I started recalling my Authentic Self and chose to live from that place.

I thanked pontoon boat for everything she shared with me.

She knew I did not want to leave.

Who would want to leave such peace?

However, the lessons were not yet finished. Pontoon said I was missing some things that were right in front of me.

The first thing I was not seeing was the Wind.

I thought that was silly, one cannot see the Wind.

But pontoon boat replied, "Just because I don't see the Wind, does not mean it is not there." She asked, "Do you feel it?"

I replied, "That's a silly question. Of course, I feel the Wind."

After some pondering, I understood. Though I could not see the Wind, I knew it was there because I felt it.

Pontoon told me as I surrender to the Wind, I would develop a knowing where to go and when to go there. She also explained I had other friends who would help me on my Journey. Some friends I would see and others I would not.

The Friends I could not see would help me indirectly by bringing boats into my life, like pontoon. At times these unseen Friends would guide me more directly.

That knowledge started to lift my loneliness. But I wanted to know more about the Ocean.

Pontoon smiled at me, knowingly. "You will learn. The mystery of the Ocean runs deep. Understanding the Ocean takes time. Be patient with yourself. This Knowledge needs to be experienced."

I was told another teacher would come into my life who would help me gain a deeper understanding. This happened sooner than I expected.

I was out on the Ocean one day, lost in thought, when I realized it had become dark.

The stars and moon were covered by clouds. I was unsure which direction to go, until I saw a bright light. I decided to follow it.

At the end of the light was a lighthouse. The lighthouse had so much Love to share. Like me, other boats were drawn to its' light.

Loneliness
Anger
Depression
Worthlessness

Other boats and I would go and listen to the lighthouse as often as possible. Through the lighthouse's words and actions, I started understanding more and more what pontoon said to me.

Over time, I just had an inner knowing of where to go and when to go there.

The lighthouse helped many to release things that kept us from being our Authentic Selves.

Many of us let go of opinions and beliefs that no longer served us.

Lighthouse helped us to see Truth, and to understand that opinions and beliefs could be true or false.

But there is only one Truth.

It takes Courage to seek Truth alone.
In doing so, it becomes easier to allow the Wind to lead.

We started releasing emotions and vibrations of words we carried for so many years. We were learning to let our emotions be felt, and understood, before allowing them to pass.

Like opinions and beliefs, it takes Courage to let go of our emotional pain and seek Truth alone.

The more I allowed the Wind to lead me, the more things changed. I was happier, even joyous.

My sail and hull were getting lighter and brighter. I was becoming less critical of others.

One funny thing about this Journey is that sometimes as old barnacles disappear, new ones appear. That is what happened to me. I got a huge new barnacle that looked like a gigantic wart.

 When I looked at my sail there was a new dark word, SPIRITUAL PRIDE.

I had been thinking that I was special because of how much I was changing. I thought I had more Wisdom than others.

I even thought I knew more than boats that had been working on their inner lives for years!

Everyone was patient with me, though; never scolding, always Loving.

The good thing about following the Wind is how much quicker I learned. Here I called myself spiritual, and yet I was looking down upon other boats who were not doing this Journey. I even thought I knew more than some of my spiritual teachers.

We are all on the same Journey, although our timelines may be different.

The more I got to know the Ocean, the more I knew unseen
Friends were all around, guiding and teaching me.

They were always there, waiting until I asked for help.

Submarine took me under the Ocean so I could see all the Friends that helped me and everyone else.

It was beautiful getting to know these unseen Guides who were always ready to help. Some of my favorites were Whale, Dolphin, Seal, although there were many more.

Anger
Loneliness
Depression
Spiritual Pride
Worthlessness

All these unseen Friends shared so much Love.
They did not judge, they Loved.

As I grew, I realized others who watched over me from faraway
lands were, just like the others, simply Loving.

It was about this time as I sailed, letting the Wind take me wherever and to whomever, that I developed a motor.

How bewildering!

As my motor started, I was led in a new direction.

I talked to some of my unseen Friends to understand what was going on.

I was happy now—I did not need a motor. When I wanted one, I did not get one, but now when I was perfectly content, I had a motor.

One of my Friends, Seal, told me that when we Journey with the Universe, we get gifts to help ourselves and others move forward. I was now able to use a motor without being selfish. That was because I had released enough of the energy of the words I carried.

(As I continue to release, my gifts develop—given by Ocean—to help others.)

I was awestruck that the great Ocean trusted me to do my part. I became excited every day, wondering where I was going and what I was going to do.

As I said at the beginning, I did not know where the Wind was taking me, didn't know and didn't care.

There is so much I went through and there is so much ahead. I love to share because we all have difficult times and beautiful times.

We all go through the Journey differently but end up in the same place. We all come out of the depths of the Ocean and return to the Ocean.

As all of us are part of the Ocean, we are not alone. We not only have each other, we are part of each other, we are part of everything.

I came into this life and experienced loneliness, and I have learned I am not alone, but part of The All, just as you are.

I have so many stories to share about the Ocean and the Love that is shared with me. I know the Ocean and the Wind will keep teaching me.

This is not the end of my story, it is just the beginning. And there is so much more to discover along the way.

Author's Afterword...

My hope is that this book brings something of soul value to all who read it.

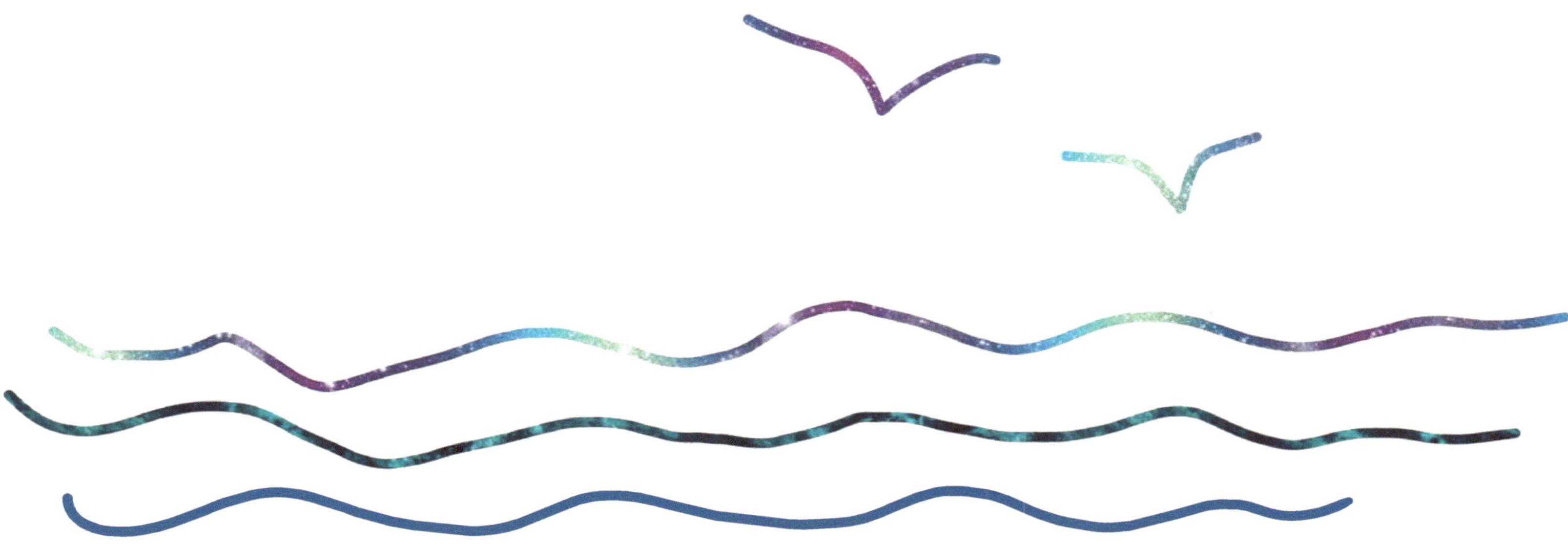

Acknowledgements

I would like to thank the following people: Larry and Tamar Schwartz, for guiding me through the publishing process; and lisa roma, for editing and layout, and making the book look as nice as it does, and for understanding the depths of Sailboat.

To Jennifer Anne, my daughter-in-law, for her beautiful portrayal of the Littlest Sailboat, and to my adult children, Chris, Nicole, and Katrina, whom I have learned so much from.
To Mother Charlotte Mary, the first mystic I got to know, and my first spiritual teacher. And, to Ron D'Amico, who has helped me get to know who I really truly AM and appreciate all the work he has done with me and the deep friendship we have developed.

I would like to thank AFSI (All Faiths Seminary International); without them, this book would not have been born.

With My Heartfelt Thanks, *Theresa Contaxis*

inger
ear
ness
epression